The Midnight Hour

Story by

Pat McGauley

Illustrated by

Rhonda Roskos

Merry Christmas

Pat McGauley

For my son, Christopher

Published by PJM Publishing
2808 Fifth Avenue West
Hibbing, MN 5576
218-262-3935
Email: shatiferin@aol.com

ISBN: 978-0-9724209-6-9

Library of Congress (EPCN) control number: 2011907786

First Edition: November, 2011

We all know that Santa Claus is a merry, jolly and kindly old man. Through the ages, his goodness has become a special part of our Christmas tradition.

We also know that Santa has to read millions of letters and make millions of toys in his magical workshop so that each special toy can be delivered to the boy or girl who asked for it. And, of course, Santa must find out "who's been naughty or nice…"

In December, as Christmas Day creeps closer, Santa worries about getting everything finished on time.

Fortunately, all of Santa's elves are good little workers and always go about their tasks with smiles on their faces. Sometimes even Mrs. Claus joins in and leads the elves in singing a Christmas song like 'Jingle Bells' as they work.

Each morning at ten o'clock, and then again in the late afternoon, the elves take a ten-minute break from their tasks to enjoy some of Mrs. Claus' delicious cookies.
Most have a glass of milk, too.

Then, it is back to work for all of them.

All of them except... Nathan!

You see, Nathan was the only unhappy elf in the entire workshop. Nobody, not even Santa, could quite understand why Nathan was always complaining. "Why do we have to make toys on Saturdays? Why can't we have a morning and afternoon nap after eating our cookies? Why can't we go out and play in the snow more often?" With Nathan, it was always one question – and one complaint – after another.

Most of the other elves ignored Nathan's whining because they were too busy, and too happy, to pay much attention to his many problems.

However, when Nathan was lazy,

all of the elves would become upset.

Abram, Benjamin and Caleb were the oldest boy elves in
Santa's workshop, while Delphina, along with Angelina and
Sapphire were the leaders of the girls' workshop.
Together they kept Santa up-to-date on every detail.

One morning, just a few days before Christmas, these six elves
had a meeting with Santa Claus.

"What can we do about Nathan, Santa?" Caleb asked. "After our cookie break, he finds a place under his work bench to hide and take a nap."

"And he always takes an extra cookie with him," added a frowning Angelina.

"Something really needs to be done about Nathan's bad behavior, Santa," Benjamin added in his squeaky voice.

Santa ran his pudgy fingers through his thick, white beard and listened as the elves complained. Of course, Santa knew all about Nathan's misbehavior because his keen eyes never missed a thing.

Now, with the elves becoming so very upset, Santa knew that the time had finally come for him to deal with the problem. A tiny tear formed in the corner of Santa's usually twinkling eyes.

"It is sad for me to say this, but Nathan just doesn't seem to enjoy being a part of our toy-making team. As much as I don't like punishments, Nathan has been too naughty, too often."

With the elves sitting on the floor, Santa explained;
"We have always been lucky to have the good angel,

Joyous,

to watch over
our workshop.
Joyous
is the reason
for the magical
things
that happen here
at the North Pole.

Miracles are needed for us to make the toys for
every boy and girl in the world." The elves nodded,
as they had all heard about Joyous.

Santa's face became very serious, "What you don't know is that there is also a bad fairy. His name is **Maldeed**. He lives alone in a place far, far away from here. No one has ever seen Maldeed, but I have heard some terrible stories about him. Perhaps the cold weather and deep snow have kept him away."

"I believe that Maldeed has somehow found his way to the North Pole. And once here, he might have put bad ideas into Nathan's head."
How that might have happened, Santa had no idea. The matter would have to be resolved because Christmas Eve was only two days away!

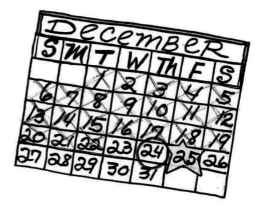

Santa took Nathan aside the next morning.
He sat the little elf on his knee, "Nathan, I must send you
to your room for the day." Santa then explained his reasons.
"Tomorrow, I will expect you to make an apology to
everybody for behaving so badly."

Nathan knew that he deserved a punishment. Santa had asked him many times to be good. Yet, the naughty elf had never been sent to his room before.

He began to cry. "I'm so very sorry, Santa. I don't like being naughty. I don't know why I am always misbehaving. I get so angry with myself for making you and the other elves unhappy." Santa nodded. "Nathan, I want you to say a prayer. Ask *Joyous,* the good angel, to help you to be good again."

Nathan went to his room and laid down on his
bed to think about all the naughty things he had done.
He would try extra hard to be a better elf tomorrow.
But, Nathan was too upset and tired to say his prayer.
He closed his eyes and in a few minutes was softly snoring.

While asleep, the voice of the bad fairy entered Nathan's
dreams. The elf tossed and turned as he listened.
"Under your pillow, Nathan, is a small bag with a magic
powder inside," Maldeed said.

"Once you awaken, put some of this powder in Santa's chocolate milk. When Santa drinks his milk, something wonderful will suddenly happen. Santa will think you are the best little elf in his workshop. Not only will Santa be happier than ever before, he will want to take you along with him in his magic sleigh on Christmas Eve."

Maldeed warned Nathan, "You must be careful that none of the other elves see what you are doing."

Of course, what wicked Maldeed told Nathan in that dream was a terrible lie! In that little bag under Nathan's pillow was a powerful sleeping powder. If Santa were to taste even the smallest amount of the powder, he would sleep for five long days.

When Nathan awoke and found the little bag, he crept downstairs and quietly slipped into the kitchen. It was still a few minutes before the morning cookie break and Santa, along with all the elves, were busy in the workshop.

Nathan hid behind the stove where the cookies were baking. He waited until Mrs. Claus was not looking.

Spotting Santa's large red cup of chocolate milk on the counter, Nathan sprinkled some powder into the cup.

Then, quickly, he tiptoed out of the kitchen, up the stairs and back into his tiny bedroom.

After his cookies and cup of chocolate milk, Santa said to Mrs. Claus, "I'm so very tired, I think that I will take a little nap. Maybe some extra sleep will do me good … because Christmas Eve is the day after tomorrow." He gave a big yawn.

"I am so tired that I might even sleep until the morning."

It was very unusual for Santa to be going to bed so early in the day, but Mrs. Claus understood. Everybody had been working so very hard these past many days.

"I will wake you in the morning, my dear," she said in her soft voice. "Be sure to cover yourself with lots of blankets so you don't catch a cold."

Well, the next morning, Mrs. Claus could not wake up her husband. She tried everything – even pouring
a glass of cold water
over his head!!

Shaking him, Mrs. Claus said, "You must wake
up my dear. It's only one day before Christmas Eve!"

But, Santa still slept soundly. Mrs. Claus was worried, but she decided to let Santa sleep until noon. The elves had lots of work to keep them busy anyhow.

At noon, she tried to awaken Santa again. Still he slept. And slept… and slept! In fact, Santa slept right through the day and through that night as well.

By now, word of Santa's endless sleep had spread among the elves. "It's Christmas Eve day!" Abram cried.

"Santa must wake up. He must! If he doesn't wake up, there will be no Christmas this year!" Little Delphina sobbed along with the rest of the girl elves.

"What can we possibly do?" asked Caleb.
"Mrs. Claus has tried shaking the bed,
pouring cold water on his head,
tickling his feet and everything
else she can think of."

"All of the good boys and girls will
be heart-broken if we can't
wake Santa up," Benjamin said
as he wiped tears from his eyes.

Nathan watched quietly from the corner.
Surely, it was that 'magic powder'
that had put Santa Claus to sleep.
He realized that he had been tricked
into doing something very bad.

But, what could he do about it now?
Nathan felt more terrible than ever
before in his life.

Christmas Eve day came. And, still Santa slept…
into the afternoon and into the early evening. It was already
becoming dark outside.

The elves had packed Santa's magic sleigh with his huge bag
full of toys. The nine reindeer, with Rudolph up in front,
were all hitched up to the sleigh and excited to make their
flight around the world.

But Santa's deep sleep continued. Then, a miracle happened!

The good angel, Joyous found Nathan alone in his bedroom.
Nathan was sobbing. Because of him, there would be
millions of disappointed children on Christmas morning.
The whole world was going to be sad,
and he was the one
person to blame.

"Listen to
me, Nathan."
Joyous sat down on the bed beside the
little elf. "I know what happened, but I don't have any
magical powers to break Maldeed's sleeping spell.
Only you can wake Santa from the 'Five Day Sleep'."
Joyous squeezed his tiny hand, "Only you can do it, Nathan!"

Nathan's eyes widened, "Oh, Good Angel, how can I awaken him? I'll do anything in the world!"

Joyous whispered in Nathan's tiny ear. "If you are absolutely sorry for what you have done and promise to be the best elf in all of the North Pole for the rest of your life – then you can break the spell on Santa Claus."

"I am absolutely sorry, Joyous. And, I promise with all my heart that I will never, never, never be naughty again. Never! I will be the merriest elf in the workshop if only I can wake up that good-hearted man!"

"Then, here is what you must do, Nathan." The angel whispered into Nathan's ear.

Nathan had to work fast, if Santa did not get his magic
sleigh off the ground in five minutes, he would never be able
to get to every rooftop in the world!

Time was running out. Mrs. Claus and the elves sat and watched the clock tick away the time.

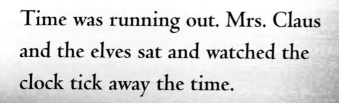

Just four minutes left!
The clock continued to tick....

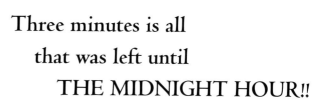

Three minutes is all
that was left until
THE MIDNIGHT HOUR!!

While they all watched the slow sweep of the minute hand on the big clock in the kitchen, Nathan crept into Santa's bedroom.

Santa was sleeping more deeply than ever. Nathan crawled onto the bed and began doing everything that Joyous had told him.

First, Nathan lifted Santa's sleeping cap and whispered into his ear…
"I'm sorry with all my heart."
Nathan was so sorry that he began to cry.

The angel had told him that if he was truly sorry, he would begin to cry.

Next,
Nathan took
one tear from each
of his eyes
and placed
a little teardrop
on each of Santa's
tightly closed
eyelids.

When Nathan did that, Santa slowly began to stir.
But, he was still sleeping!

In the kitchen, the clock was still ticking...

...Two minutes!

All of the elves were sobbing now and thinking that Christmas was surely lost!

Mrs. Claus slipped quietly away from the sad group of elves.
She would sit by Santa's bedside until he finally woke up.

But, like everybody else, Mrs. Claus had a broken heart.

When she opened the
bedroom door,
Mrs. Claus was very surprised
to see Nathan sitting
on Santa's bed.
What was that naughty
Nathan up to now,
she wondered?

Before she could say a word, however, Nathan stood on the
bed and looked down on sleeping Santa. "I will be the best
elf in the world !!!" Nathan shouted it at the top of his voice
just as Joyous had told him to do.

Nathan's promise was so loud that all the elves in the kitchen could hear him.

Even the reindeer outside could hear him.

All of a sudden...
Santa's tired eyes opened.
"My goodness!! What time is it? What day is it? And Nathan! What are you doing, standing on top of my bed?"

Santa was very confused. He asked Mrs. Claus, "How long have I been sleeping?"

"It's Christmas Eve, Santa!" Nathan blurted in excitement.

"And it's one minute until the hour of midnight strikes, my dear Santa," Mrs. Claus said in an excited voice.

But Santa's eyes were sparkling now. "I'm wide awake and ready to go!"

Nathan leaped from the bed. "What can I do to help you, Santa?"

"Quick, Nathan, get my boots, and Mrs. Claus … please find my stocking cap and warm mittens." Nathan was back in a flash, carrying the large black boots.

Mrs. Claus helped Santa slip into his fluffy red coat while Nathan tied the boot laces.

After buckling the black belt around his huge tummy, Santa gave Mrs. Claus a quick kiss on her cheek...

...and Nathan, a pat on his little head!

"Well, everybody, I'm ready to go!"
Santa shouted, in his merriest voice.
Into the kitchen Santa raced...
"Please close the door
behind me, my dear
little elves," Santa said,
as he grabbed a cookie
from the plate
on the table,
gave a wink,
and waved goodbye
to all!

"HO!...HO!...HO!"

Only a moment before midnight, Santa had rushed out of
the door and into the snowy night. He called out to his waiting
reindeer, "Let's go. On Dasher, on Dancer, on Prancer, on
Vixen, on Comet, on Cupid, on Donner and Blitzen…"

Up in front of the eight reindeer, of course, was that shining
red nose to lead them off into the night. "You, too, Rudolph.
We will really have to fly fast tonight!" Santa called.

Back at the workshop window, the elves were jumping with joy as they watched Santa's sleigh disappear into the night.

Mrs. Claus brought a fresh tray of cookies into the room.
All the elves were singing and dancing and celebrating.
"We have someone to thank for all this." Mrs. Claus said with a big smile. Hiding behind her big green apron was Nathan.

The elves listened as Nathan told them about everything that had happened. "I did something very bad…" Mrs. Claus interrupted the elf, "But then he did something very good!" She picked up Nathan and held him in her arms. "So, when Nathan told Santa that he was going to be the best elf in the world, Santa finally woke up."

Abram and Caleb led all the elves in shouting, "Hooray for Nathan! Hooray! Hooray!"

"He's the greatest!" said Delphina, with her bright smile.

From that night on, until this very day, Nathan has kept his promise. Nathan's hard work has made everybody especially happy.

In fact, each year Santa gives a golden star to the 'Number One Elf' and Nathan has more stars than any other elf in the workshop.

So, my friends, that's the
"STORY OF A CHRISTMAS
THAT ALMOST DIDN'T HAPPEN."
But, that was many, many years ago.
....and, if you were wondering...
the bad fairy, Maldeed, has never again returned to the magical
land of the North Pole.

ABOUT THE AUTHOR

Pat McGauley is a former schoolteacher and author of six published novels. This is his third children's story. Previously, he has written: *Mazral and Derisa (An Easter Story)* and *Santa The King*. Both are available through PJM Publishing. McGauley lives in Minnesota and Florida.

ABOUT THE ILLUSTRATOR

Rhonda Roskos, is an award-winning artist living in Grand Rapids, Minn. with her husband, Wayne. Although widely recognized for her paintings, THE MIDNIGHT HOUR is Rhonda's first book project.